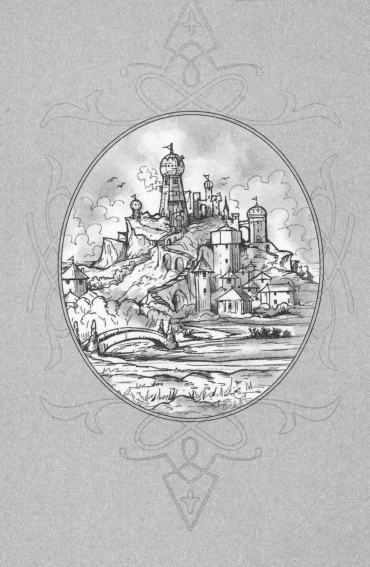

of **Wrenly**

Flatfrost

Primlox

Bogburp

The
Mainland

Trellis

The Stone Forest

Hobsgrove

The Kingdom of Wrenly

of

17

Goblin Magic

WITHDRAWN

By Jordan Quinn
Illustrated by Robert McPhillips

LITTLE SIMON
New York   London   Toronto   Sydney   New Delhi

LITTLE SIMON

An imprint of Simon & Schuster Children's Publishing Division

1230 Avenue of the Americas, New York, New York 10020

First Little Simon paperback edition December 2021

Copyright © 2021 by Simon & Schuster, Inc.

Also available in a Little Simon hardcover edition.

All rights reserved, including the right of reproduction in whole or in part in any form.

LITTLE SIMON is a registered trademark of Simon & Schuster, Inc., and associated colophon is a trademark of Simon & Schuster, Inc.

For information about special discounts for bulk purchases, please contact Simon & Schuster Special Sales at 1-866-506-1949 or business@simonandschuster.com.

The Simon & Schuster Speakers Bureau can bring authors to your live event. For more information or to book an event contact the Simon & Schuster Speakers Bureau at 1-866-248-3049 or visit our website at www.simonspeakers.com.

Manufactured in the United States of America 1121 MTN

2 4 6 8 10 9 7 5 3 1

Library of Congress Cataloging-in-Publication Data

Names: Quinn, Jordan, author. | McPhillips, Robert, 1971– illustrator. | Quinn, Jordan. Kingdom of Wrenly ; 17. | Title: Goblin magic / by Jordan Quinn ; illustrated by Robert McPhillips. | Description: First Little Simon edition. | New York : Little Simon, an imprint of Simon & Schuster Children's Publishing Division, 2021. | Series: The kingdom of Wrenly ; 17 | Summary: The people of Wrenly have always believed that goblins are dangerous creatures who were stripped of their magical powers by wizards after the Goblin Battles; and when Prince Lucas and Clara follow a young goblin, Zark, who has come from the wizard Grom, they find themselves captured by the goblin leader, Golart, who has taken over Hobsgrove—but Grom has a plan, and it requires that the children put their trust in Zark. | Identifiers: LCCN 2021011615 (print) | LCCN 2021011616 (ebook) | ISBN 9781534495531 (paperback) | ISBN 9781534495548 (hardcover) | ISBN 9781534495555 (v. 17 ; ebook) | Subjects: LCSH: Goblins—Juvenile fiction. | Wizards—Juvenile fiction. | Magic—Juvenile fiction. | Trust—Juvenile fiction. | Friendship—Juvenile fiction. | Imaginary places—Juvenile fiction. | CYAC: Goblins—Fiction. | Wizards—Fiction. | Magic—Fiction. | Trust—Fiction. | Friendship—Fiction. | Classification: LCC PZ7.Q31945 Go 2021(print) | LCC PZ7.Q31945(ebook) | DDC [Fic]—dc23 LC record available at https://lccn.loc.gov/2021011615

CONTENTS

CHAPTER 1

Chore Loser!

Cock-a-doodle-doo! crowed the village rooster. Clara Gills dragged her pillow down over her head.

Cock-a-doodle-doo!

This time Clara groaned. *Why is getting up SO hard?* she thought. Doing her early morning chores every day never seemed to get easier.

Clara slid out of bed and pulled on her trousers, tunic, and boots.

The smell of freshly baked bread wafted up from under her door. "Mmm," she murmured. The sweet, delicious aroma coming from her dad's bakery always made her perk up in the morning.

Clara left her bedroom and walked down the wooden stairs.

"Good morning, Father!" she said, grabbing a hot biscuit.

Her father slid a large wooden paddle into the stone oven. "Good morning!"

Clara nibbled on her biscuit and sipped a cup of tea while her father unloaded more bread from the oven.

Then, after she finished eating, she filled the display counter with warm loaves.

Meanwhile, at the royal stables, Clara's best friend, Prince Lucas, was doing his morning chores too. First he mucked and raked the stalls.

Then he spread fresh wood shavings across the floor. After that he refilled the feeding tubs and water buckets for the horses.

Clara, who had arrived after finishing her own chores, poked her head into the barn.

"Morning! Are you almost done?"
The prince hung up his pitchfork
and turned around.

"I am now!" Lucas said, smiling.

"Great, me too. Let's get our
horses ready for our training!" Clara
cried.

The kids quickly saddled up their horses, Ivan and Scallop, and led them to the riding ring.

It was time to go around the jumping course their instructor had prepared. After a few laps Lucas looked over at his friend.

"I have an idea. Are you up for a race? Winner has to do the other person's chores for a *whole* week."

Clara narrowed her eyes. "Deal. You're ON!"

Lucas and Clara led their horses to the starting mark inside the arena. Then they crouched in their saddles and waited.

"*Ready? Set! GO!*" shouted Lucas.

And just like that, the kids took
off. They galloped around the track
as fast as they could.

But just as they rounded the last
curve, Clara suddenly pulled in front
and crossed the finish line first.

"Woo-hoo! I WIN!" she cried. "Have fun helping my father at the bakery!"

Lucas had tried his best, but he knew a deal was a deal.

And the way he saw it, he hadn't really lost. Eating butternut bread for breakfast all week was going to be a tasty treat.

CHAPTER 2

Daily Classes

After their horse riding lesson, Lucas and Clara ran to the archery glen for shooting practice.

Clara grabbed a quiver of arrows and loaded her bow. Lucas did the same, and they stood side by side, facing their targets.

Clara exhaled and steadied her bow. Her hand lightly rubbed the side of her face.

Then *whoosh!* She let the arrow go.
It zoomed ahead until . . . *WHACK!*
The sharp tip of the arrow landed
on the bull's-eye.

Lucas bit his lip and loaded his bow too. He focused as hard as he could. *Whoosh!* His arrow launched forward but hit the outer edge of the target.

"Argh!" groaned the prince. He quickly loaded another arrow and let it fly. But this time it went too far and disappeared into the forest.

Meanwhile, Clara took another perfect shot.

Whiz! Thwack! The sharp tip hit the inner circle of the target.

"Seriously, do you *ever* miss?" Lucas cried. "How are you so good?"

Clara turned to the prince. "You have strong arms. I know you can do it too," she said. "You just need more discipline."

Lucas knew she was right. But he secretly wondered if Clara practiced when he wasn't around.

For now, he was glad to hang up his bow. It was time to go back to the castle for history, one of Lucas's favorite subjects.

He'd been looking forward to reading about the Enchanted Goblin Battles.

"Wow, goblins were dangerous," Clara whispered to Lucas.

"They used to be," said the prince. "I've read that before the Goblin Battles broke out, they used their magic without limits and endangered our kingdom."

Clara looked down at a drawing in her book. The goblins had bat-like ears, long hooked noses, short torsos, and large glowing eyes.

"I wonder if goblins still look like this."

"I think they might, but no one knows for sure," Lucas replied. "All goblins were stripped of their magical powers. They haven't been seen in years."

Goblin

"Wow, you really get into this history stuff," Clara said. "For me, I'm just glad goblins don't bother us anymore."

Lucas and Clara then shelved their history books and hurried off to their potions class, which was taught by the great, and somewhat grumpy, wizard Grom.

The kids didn't enjoy making potions. The mixtures they made smelled disgusting with a capital D.

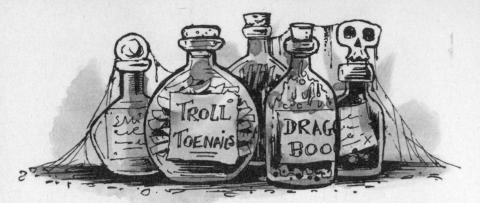

And no wonder! The ingredients they had to stomach were strange things like troll toenails, dragon boogers, bat drool, slime of slugs, cobwebs, and swamp water.

"Get ready to gag," said Lucas as they wound down the spiral stairs.

But when they opened the door, Grom was nowhere in sight. Instead, a mysterious hooded figure stood in front of them.

CHAPTER 3

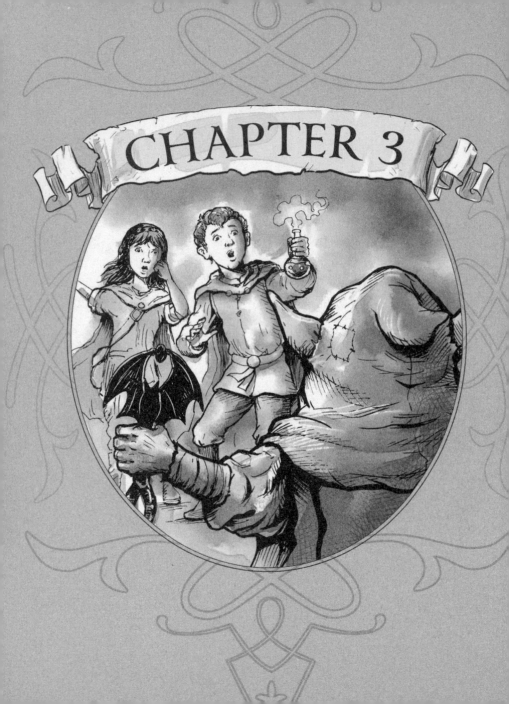

The Message

"Oh my!" cried Clara. "There's an intruder in the castle!"

Lucas picked up a potion bottle and held it in the air, ready to open it to distract their unwanted guest.

"Stand back!" Lucas yelled out.

The hooded figure quickly shielded himself with his arms. "Please don't hurt me!" he exclaimed. "I mean no harm!"

"Tell us who you are and how you got into this castle first," Lucas demanded.

So the hooded stranger slowly lowered his arms and showed his face.

Clara gasped as she and Lucas both shook their heads in disbelief.

The trespasser standing in front of them had large batlike ears, a hooked nose, and large green glowing eyes, just like the picture in their history book. There was no mistaking they were face-to-face with a young goblin.

"Your potions teacher, Grom, sent me," he explained. "He told me how to find the hidden key to this room."

Then the goblin took out a crystal from his pocket and held it in front of them. "The wizards of Wrenly are in danger."

Lucas clutched the crystal with his free hand. The moment he touched the gem, a beam of light shot up as a hologram appeared.

"It's a message from Grom!" cried Clara as they leaned in to listen.

"Hello, Prince Lucas, if you are watching this, we have grave trouble on Hobsgrove," the wizard began.

"More trouble than all of us can handle—"

Right then the image began to cut out, and the kids could only catch broken phrases.

"A powerful danger to Wrenly," they heard Grom say. "Help us . . . *DO NOT BRING THE KING* . . . goblin magic . . ." Then the crystal cracked and the message was gone.

"Oh no!" cried the prince. "What do we do now?"

The goblin pointed toward the door. "You must come to Hobsgrove with me," he said. "A boat is waiting."

Lucas looked to his best friend, who nodded. Then the prince looked sternly at the goblin.

"We will go with you, but you must stay out of sight. Meet us at the royal stables," he said.

The goblin nodded firmly as he made his exit. Lucas and Clara waited until the castle guards weren't looking, and then they ran to the royal stables. When they got there, the mysterious goblin was already waiting for them behind a bush.

"Where's the boat?" Lucas whispered.

The goblin covered his head with the hood of his cloak. "On the other side of the woods," he replied.

Then he led the way until they arrived at the edge of the sea.

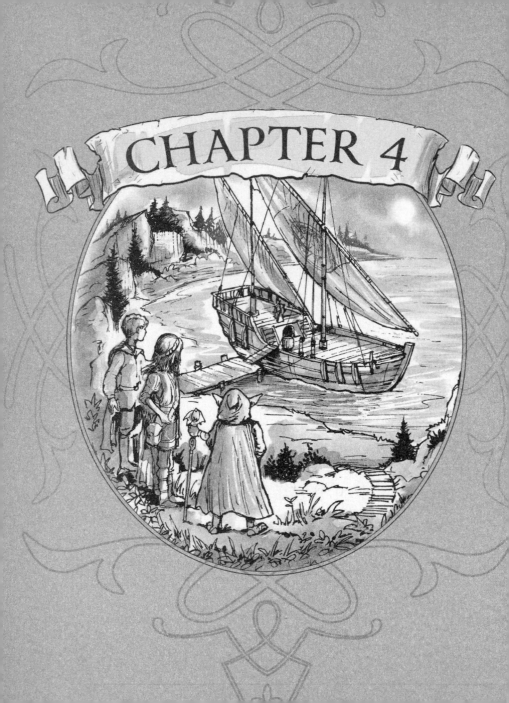

CHAPTER 4

A Friendly Voyage

A wizard's ship was waiting for them in a quiet, hidden cove. Lucas believed that the young goblin was sent by Grom, but still, he felt uneasy.

Clara leaned in close to the prince. "Don't worry. We're doing the right thing," she whispered. Lucas held her gaze and let out a sigh. He felt better knowing his best friend felt the same way he did.

The kids got on the ship as the goblin hoisted the sails and untied the boat from the dock. They were on their way to Hobsgrove, the island of wizards.

Once they were settled in, Lucas realized they didn't know their goblin messenger's name.

"I'm Prince Lucas, and this is my friend Clara Gills," he offered. "What is *your* name?"

The goblin kept his eyes focused on the water, giving no answer.

Clara pressed her knee against the prince's leg. Were they going to have to sit in awkward silence the entire time?

But finally the goblin spoke. "My name is Zark."

The kids waited for him to say more, but again he said nothing.

"This is the first time we've met a goblin like yourself," Lucas prodded.

Zark turned the wheel and looked up at the sails. "Well, I've never met a human before, either. I've only heard horrible things."

Lucas and Clara nudged each other again. The conversation was going from bad to worse.

"Well, we've never heard anything good about *goblins*, either," Lucas zinged back.

Again they sailed on in silence until Zark turned and looked sharply at the prince.

"Is it really true that humans and wizards will do anything for power?"

Lucas shifted uncomfortably. He and Clara had just read about how goblins were punished and stripped of their magic.

"Well, I know why you might think that," he said. "But after the Goblin Battles, the wizards needed to protect our kingdom."

Prince Lucas could tell the goblin was searching for the right words.

"My hope is that one day we will be trusted and magic will be restored to us," he replied. "We may not have magic, but we still practice the art of potion-making to heal our kind."

Lucas and Clara scrunched their faces. And Zark actually chuckled.

"Yes, potions smell *disgusting*, especially ones mixed with troll toenails."

This time they all laughed.

"So what else do goblins like you do?" asked Clara. "Do you like archery?"

Zark shook his head. "Not really. Goblins don't have great eyesight."

Lucas was glad to hear he wasn't the only one who didn't care for the sport.

"What about history?" he chimed in eagerly.

Zark shrugged. "No. After all, history hasn't been kind to us."

"I'm sorry to hear that," Lucas said with a pause. "In meeting you, we now know that goblins must be kind and brave."

Zark smiled at Lucas. Then he turned to guide the ship to the shore of Hobsgrove.

As soon as they landed, Lucas and Clara helped Zark secure the boat to the dock. In the distance, a strange thumping sound was getting louder and louder.

A horde of goblins was coming toward them! And they did *not* look friendly at all.

51

CHAPTER 5

Prisoners

"Seize them!" the goblin leader shouted. The goblin army quickly surrounded Lucas and Clara.

Zark shook his head in disbelief. *"No-o-o!"* he wailed helplessly as the kids were taken away.

Everything happened so fast. But from the panicked look on Zark's face, Clara guessed that this had not been part of his plan.

"Take them to the dungeon!" the head goblin cried.

So his goblin soldiers pushed them along and forced the kids into the wizard's castle—a place where they would normally be welcome. They were led down a dark, musty stairwell and were pushed behind an iron gate.

Lucas and Clara fell to their knees.

"Prince Lucas!" came a voice from the dark.

Then the figure revealed himself. It was Grom.

The kids got up and brushed themselves off.

Grom held up a torch. The kids could see he wasn't alone. *All* the wizards had been captured.

"Are you both all right?" Grom asked.

Lucas and Clara nodded.

Grom sighed. "Thank you for coming to help us," he said. "Golart, the goblin leader, has taken over Hobsgrove." Lucas thought back to the army that had captured them.

"He knew
our prison was
strong enough
to hold wizards.
Our magic does
not work here,"
Grom explained.

Golart

"Golart wants to take over the entire
kingdom and regain goblin magic."

Lucas knew the wizard dungeon
had a powerful spell over it. It was
meant to hold evil sorcerers or
anyone who brought harm. But it
was never meant to imprison *good*
wizards.

The prince looked up and scanned the cell.

"Who is *she*?" he asked, referring to the woman in their midst.

Grom held the torch in front of him. "This is Anora, the new leader of Hobsgrove."

Lucas and Clara bowed before her. Anora nodded as Lucas turned back to Grom. "What can we do to help?"

Grom shined the torch on a dark corner of the dungeon. "We've been waiting for you because we have a plan."

Lucas and Clara followed the wizard across the dirt floor. Anora followed too. Grom stopped and held the torch over a drain. With his free hand, he pulled off the grate.

"Below this drain is a passageway," the wizard explained. "The opening is too small for us, but you and Clara should have no problem."

Lucas stuck his head inside and studied the drain. "And what do we do once we get down there?"

Anora pulled a scroll from her sleeve. "Here is a map," she said. "Follow it to a winding staircase that will lead you to the potion room."

Grom rested his hand on the prince's shoulder. "In that room, you'll have to find the spell that reverses the dungeon's protection spell. There was never a need to reverse it until now. Do you both understand what you need do?"

Lucas and Clara nodded gravely.

"Yes, we do," said the prince. "And we won't let you down."

CHAPTER 6

The Secret Passageway

Clara sat on the edge of the drain and slowly lowered her legs into the opening. She twisted one way and then the other until her body slipped through.

"I'm okay!" she called from below. "But it's *very* dark down here."

Lucas lay on his stomach and lowered a torch into the opening. Clara grabbed ahold of it.

Then the prince shimmied down
after her.

Ker-plunk! He landed on his
bottom. Clara tried hard not to
laugh. The prince made a face as he
stood up. Then he unrolled the map,
held it to the light, and studied it.

They had a long way to go.

"We're standing *here*," he said, pointing to the drain's entryway. "And this is the main tunnel, which leads to the winding staircase and up to the potions room."

He rolled up the map and shoved it into his back pocket.

"Come on. Let's go!"

The torch flickered eerily on the damp walls. Rats scuttled into the nooks and crannies on either side of the tunnel.

Soon they came to the winding staircase. At the end of it, there was an arched door made of timber. The door had two iron hinges and a heavy latch. Lucas pushed up to lift it.

"Oh no! It's locked!"

But that's when Clara spied a bronze key hanging on a hook beside the door. She lifted the key and held it out in front of the prince.

"But, luckily, we're not locked *out!*"

Clara rushed to fit the key in as Lucas held the torch above them.

With one turn, the secret passageway opened. The kids slowly walked into the grand potions room and looked up in awe.

There were shelves filled with books and counters lined with bottles of all shapes and sizes. The room had a hearth, cauldrons, and a long oak table with a scale on it.

"Wow!" exclaimed Lucas. "This is the room that holds *all* the secrets of Hobsgrove!"

Clara looked around at the potions that lined the walls. "And somewhere in here is the dungeon's reversal spell!"

The kids got right to work. Clara studied the labels on the potions and elixirs. Lucas paged through invisibility spells, spells for magical creatures, and even spells that could stop time.

And then he found it: *The Magical Dungeon Reversal Spell.*

"Here it is!" cried Lucas. Clara ran to the prince's side.

They had begun to read over the spell when Clara suddenly looked up from the book.

"I hear footsteps!" she whispered. "Somebody's coming!"

Lucas and Clara ducked below the table just as the door to the potions room creaked open.

"I *know* you're in here!" a familiar voice said.

The kids didn't answer.

"I promise I'm only here to help."

Lucas and Clara slowly stood up. And there, standing before them, was Zark.

CHAPTER 7

Ka-Boom!

"This is a *trap!*" the prince warned.

Zark put his hand on his heart as he lowered his hood.

"No, I swear it's not," he said. "Please let me help."

Clara thought back to how upset Zark was when the goblin army had seized them. Without Zark's warning, they would never have known the wizards were in trouble.

Lucas was still on his guard, but Clara pulled him aside to remind him that Grom trusted this young goblin too.

So the kids turned back around as Zark stood still, staring at the floor.

"Okay, we'll trust you," the prince said. "And since you're good at potions, we need your help mixing this reversal spell that will save the wizards."

Zark's face lit up. "Let's get to work!" he cried with a big smile.

"I'll read the ingredients out loud," Lucas directed as he showed Zark the spell, "while you both go find them."

Clara and Zark nodded eagerly.

"Okay, here goes," the prince began. "'One jug of witch's brew, five cups of star anise, one jar of dragon's breath, two troll toenails, and one strand of goblin hair.'"

Clara and Zark ran around the potions room, gathering the ingredients. It was like a scavenger hunt—only much more serious.

Meanwhile, Lucas set a cauldron over a fire in the hearth. One by one, Clara and Zark added the elements to the cauldron. Then Zark plucked the last ingredient—a hair from his own head.

"Here's proof that I only came to help." Then he dropped the strand of hair into the potion. Right away the mix began to gurgle.

Lucas picked up the spell book. "'Mix the ingredients until well blended,'" he read.

Clara grabbed a large wooden spoon and began to stir. The potion smelled worse than the swamps of Bogburp.

"Now chant the following spell." Lucas held his nose as Zark spoke:

Deep within the cauldron's well
Brews a bubbling foul smell.
Stir the mix and blend it well.
Now reverse the dungeon's spell.

As soon as the goblin finished, the potion began to churn and boil fiercely.

"Oh no, it's going to BLOW!" shouted Zark, pushing Lucas and Clara out of the way.

KA-BOOOOM!

The castle shook violently, and the potion rose from the cauldron like a fountain and hit Zark. All the torches blew out, and the room went dark.

Clara lit a torch from the flame beneath the cauldron—the only light in the room—and held it over him.

"Oh no, Zark is hurt!" Lucas said, grabbing him over his shoulder.

Then the kids hurried up the stone stairs to look for help.

CHAPTER 8

The Standoff

The castle was empty of both wizards *and* goblins. Lucas and Clara raced to the gatehouse and peered outside.

"I see them!" cried Lucas. Golart and the entire goblin army stood facing the wizards and Anora.

"Look! The reversal spell worked, and the wizards are free!" Clara cried.

"Hang in there, Zark," said Lucas. "We'll get you help as soon as we can."

Zark squirmed and moaned in the prince's arms.

Out in the field, Golart held a dazzling golden scepter in one hand. The top was bejeweled with gemstones.

"Oh no!" Prince Lucas cried as he watched Golart shake the magical scepter in the air. "He stole that from Grom!"

92

"Don't come closer!" Golart yelled. "Or I'll destroy you and all of Hobsgrove!"

But Grom ignored Golart's threat and stepped forward.

"I'm warning you, Golart. That scepter is very powerful. In the wrong hands it can be deadly," Grom said.

The goblin leader erupted in evil laughter. "Your magic is now mine!" he cried as a bolt of electricity blazed from the tip of the scepter. But Grom raised his arm at once.

ZAP! The magic backfired and hit one of the goblin soldiers instead.

Golart looked down in shock and started shaking it as Grom boldly took another step closer.

"Surrender now before you hurt your entire army."

Golart pounded the bottom of the scepter on the ground. "NEVER!" he boomed.

The kids watched helplessly from their hiding spot in the gatehouse.

"What should we do?" whispered Clara.

Lucas wasn't sure, but Zark was running out of time. Now there was only *one* thing to do.

"Hurry! We have to go onto the battlefield!" declared the prince. "Zark needs help *now*."

Clara squeezed her hands into two fists. "You're right," she said, mustering courage. "Let's go!"

Then the two friends ran out the
door and into the middle of the chaos.

Goblin Magic!

Lucas ran through the crowd and pulled on Anora's robe.

"Zark needs your help! Please!" the prince cried.

In that moment all the wizards and goblins stopped and watched in wonder. The young goblin was hurt and needed attention. Anora immediately took Zark in her arms and began to chant a healing spell.

"STOP the wizard now!" Golart shouted to his army. "Zark is a traitor! He's on the side of the wizards and humans, who have cursed us for years!"

Anora paid no attention to Golart's threats and continued to chant her spell.

Earth below!
Sky above!
Bind these wounds
With healing love!

Then she waved a hand over Zark. The goblin opened his eyes and sat up. The first thing he saw was Golart.

"Traitor!" Golart shouted as electricity burst from the scepter. This time it didn't bounce back.

The bolt struck Zark with great force. But instead of knocking him down, the magical blast surged through his body.

Zark then gathered the electricity into a ball with his bare hands, creating a protective force field around the kids and the rest of the wizards.

Zark shot into the air and rocketed toward Golart, snatching the scepter out of his hand. Then the young goblin flew it back to Grom, its rightful owner.

With his scepter returned, Grom
was ready to step in. He opened his
hands, and a ball of magical light
formed at the tip of the staff. He
looked straight ahead and hurled the
balls at Golart and his army. The
light encircled them, binding them in
magical chains.

109

Zark called out to Golart as he watched on.

"I've always wanted magic and equality restored to us," he said. "But not *your* way, Golart. Not all goblins are like you and your army."

Zark stood tall, with the kids, Anora, Grom, and all the Hobsgrove wizards behind him.

"From this day forward, and forevermore," Anora declared boldly, "goblin magic will *only* be used as a force for good." Then she ordered the goblin prisoners to be taken to the dungeon.

CHAPTER 10

Magic Lessons

"Zark, Prince Lucas, and Clara, thank you for your bravery," said Anora. "You saved us all. It takes strength to stand up to your enemies and even *greater* strength to stand up to your own kind."

Zark bowed in gratitude as Lucas and Clara gave each other a hug.

"I knew you two would be able to complete the mission," Grom said.

"And I knew I could trust you, too, Zark. With magic now running through your veins, you are very powerful. Would you like to train with me in the ways of magic?"

Zark looked up with a sparkle in his eye. "Thank you. I accept your kind offer with pleasure," he said.

"And the sooner I get started, the better. But first I must report back to the rest of my family. There are plenty of good goblins living in the outskirts of Wrenly."

Anora nodded. "We must send you home with a potion that will restore magical powers for everyone," she said.

With that, Zark bowed in deep gratitude.

"I've spent my whole life believing humans and wizards were not to be trusted," he said. "But deep down I've always hoped to find goodness in all."

The prince offered his hand to Zark. They shook on it and then hugged.

"Yes, we must continue to build trust between goblins and all who live in our kingdom," said the prince. "What happened here today is only the beginning. We cannot change the past, but together, we *can* change the future."

Grom rested his hand on the prince's shoulders.

"You're beginning to sound more like a *king* than a prince, Your Majesty."

Lucas blushed. He had meant every word.

Change wasn't going to happen overnight. But if there was one thing he and Clara were reminded of through their new goblin friend, it was that bravery and strength was deep inside each of them.

Being brave and standing up for what is right wouldn't be easy.

But in moments of doubt, if they learned to trust their gut and help each other, the entire kingdom would be a safe and welcome place for all.